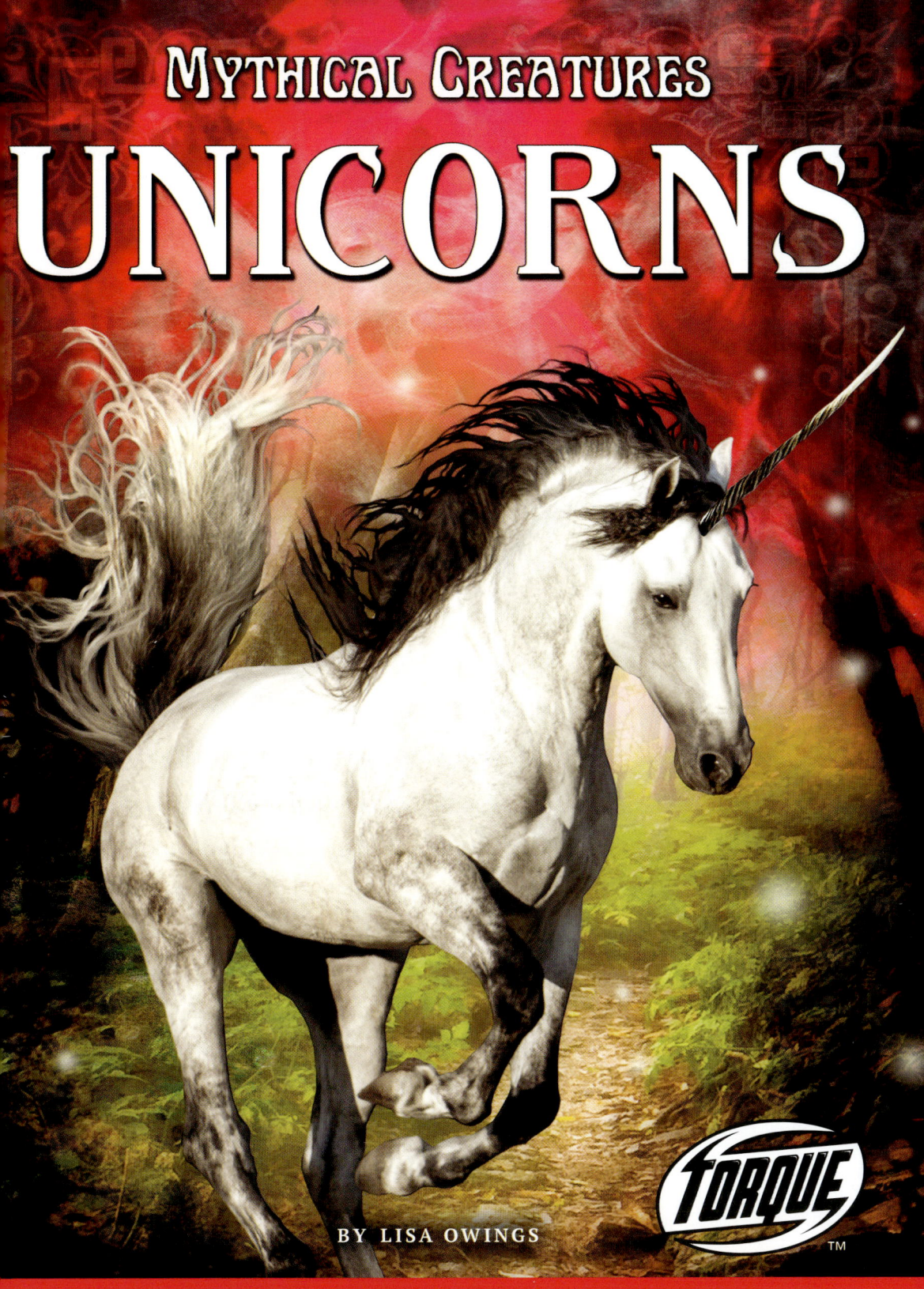

Torque brims with excitement perfect for thrill-seekers of all kinds. Discover daring survival skills, explore uncharted worlds, and marvel at mighty engines and extreme sports. In *Torque* books, anything can happen. Are you ready?

This edition first published in 2021 by Bellwether Media, Inc.
No part of this publication may be reproduced in whole or in part without written permission of the publisher.
For information regarding permission, write to Bellwether Media, Inc., Attention: Permissions Department,
6012 Blue Circle Drive, Minnetonka, MN 55343.

Library of Congress Cataloging-in-Publication Data

Names: Owings, Lisa, author.
Title: Unicorns / by Lisa Owings.
Description: Minneapolis, MN : Bellwether Media, Inc., 2021. | Series: Torque: mythical creatures | Includes bibliographical references and index. | Audience: Ages 7-12 | Audience: Grades 4-6 | Summary: "Engaging images accompany information about unicorns. The combination of high-interest subject matter and light text is intended for students in grades 3 through 7"–Provided by publisher.
Identifiers: LCCN 2020014867 (print) | LCCN 2020014868 (ebook) | ISBN 9781644872789 (library binding) | ISBN 9781681037417 (ebook)
Subjects: LCSH: Unicorns–Juvenile literature.
Classification: LCC GR830.U6 O95 2021 (print) | LCC GR830.U6 (ebook) | DDC 398/.469–dc23
LC record available at https://lccn.loc.gov/2020014867
LC ebook record available at https://lccn.loc.gov/2020014868or

Text copyright © 2021 by Bellwether Media, Inc. TORQUE and associated logos are trademarks and/or registered trademarks of Bellwether Media, Inc.

Editor: Rebecca Sabelko   Designer: Josh Brink

Printed in the United States of America, North Mankato, MN.

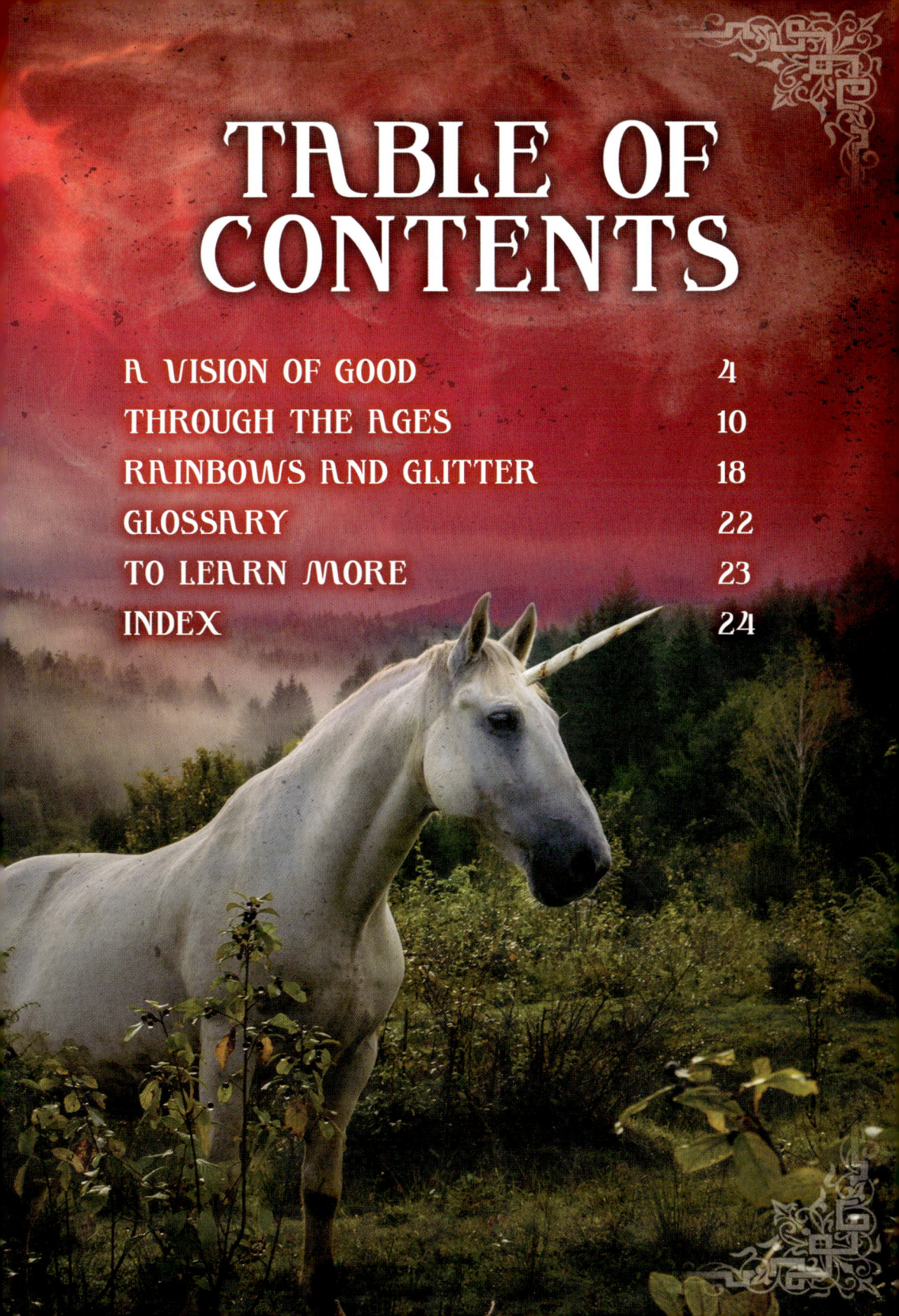

TABLE OF CONTENTS

A VISION OF GOOD	4
THROUGH THE AGES	10
RAINBOWS AND GLITTER	18
GLOSSARY	22
TO LEARN MORE	23
INDEX	24

A Vision of Good

The unicorn gallops through the forest. Hunters follow its tracks. But the unicorn knows the hunters cannot catch it.

Finally, the unicorn stops beside a hidden stream. A young girl is resting there. The unicorn lays next to her and rests its head in her lap. She strokes its **mane**. It is safe for now.

Magic Horn

People believed unicorn horns could turn water clear and clean. In stories, unicorns often dipped their horns in dirty water so other animals could safely drink.

Unicorns have **enchanted** people for more than 2,000 years. These horselike creatures sometimes have the traits of other animals. Unicorns are usually white. A single horn sprouts from the forehead.

Unicorns are **symbols** of goodness and **purity**. They stand for bravery in the face of greed and **betrayal**. They are also fast, strong, and **fierce**.

Scotland's Unicorn

The unicorn has been a national symbol of Scotland since the 1100s. The creature was chosen for its goodness and bravery!

In stories, unicorns are often hunted for their horns. Their horns are said to have healing powers and protect people from poison.

But unicorns are nearly impossible to catch. Only young girls can **tame** them. Girls are often used to attract and trap unicorns. Soon the rare creatures meet their fate.

The Horn That Cures All

During the Middle Ages, wealthy people often turned to unicorn horns, or *alicorns*, to cure sickness. Doctors claimed they could heal everything from deadly viruses to deadly bites.

THROUGH THE AGES

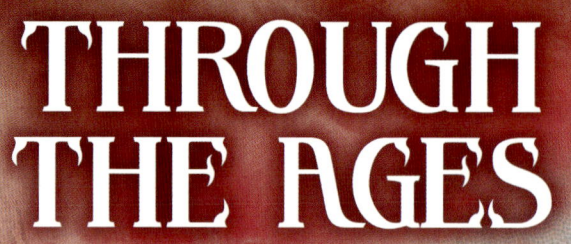

qilin

Unicorn **myths** began in Asia and Europe around 400 BCE. The *qilin*, or Chinese unicorn, had a deer's body with colorful scales. It was a symbol of good luck.

Greek historian Ctesias described a single-horned animal. It had a white body, a red head, and blue eyes. Its horn had bands of white, black, and red.

Unicorn Origin

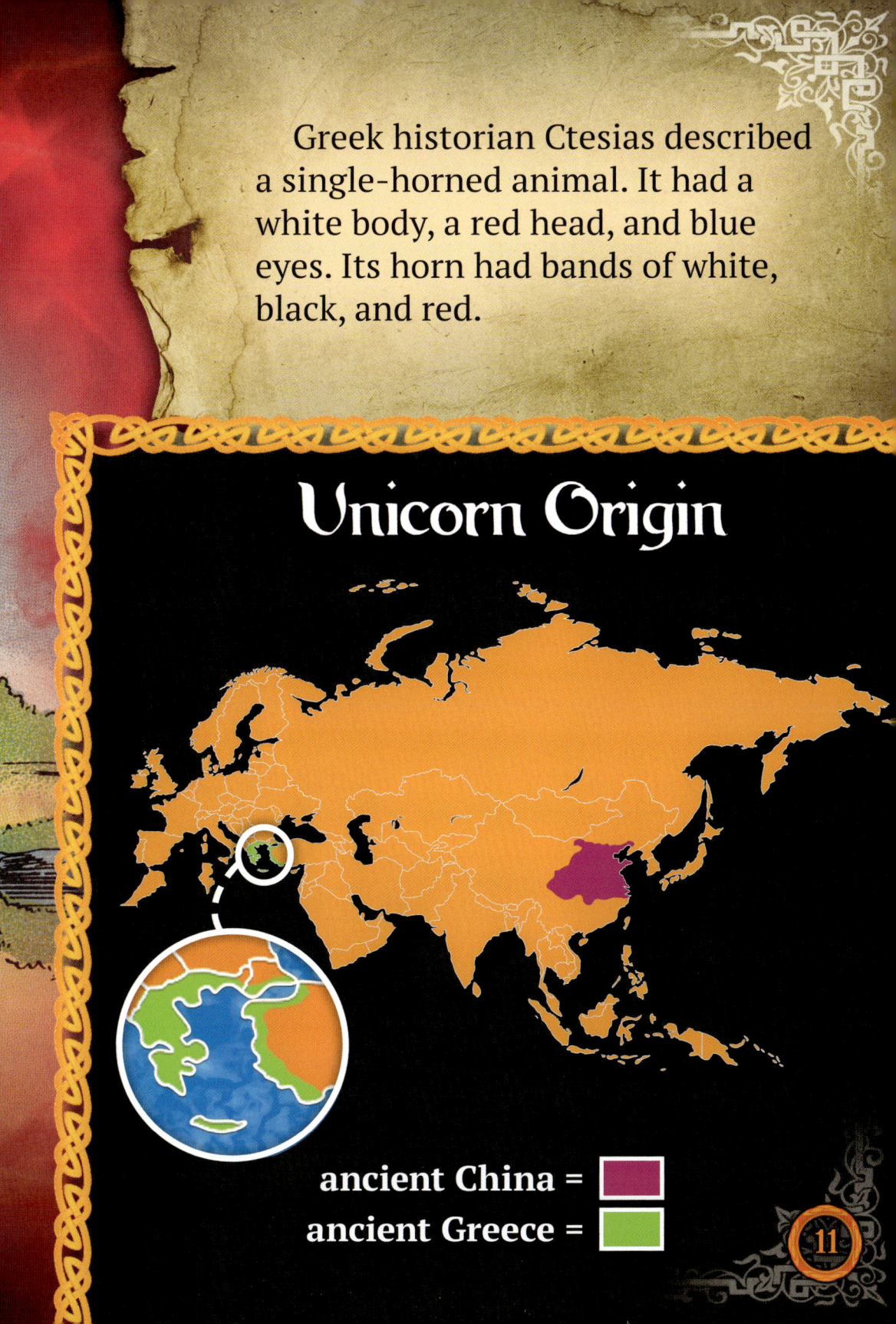

ancient China =
ancient Greece =

Unicorn stories changed over time. The Roman writer Pliny the Elder described a monoceros in 77 CE. It had a deer's body with elephant feet and one long, black horn. The animal was fierce. It could not be captured alive.

The Russian edinorog was gentle but strong. It could dig tunnels with its horn. It was said to cause earthquakes!

monoceros

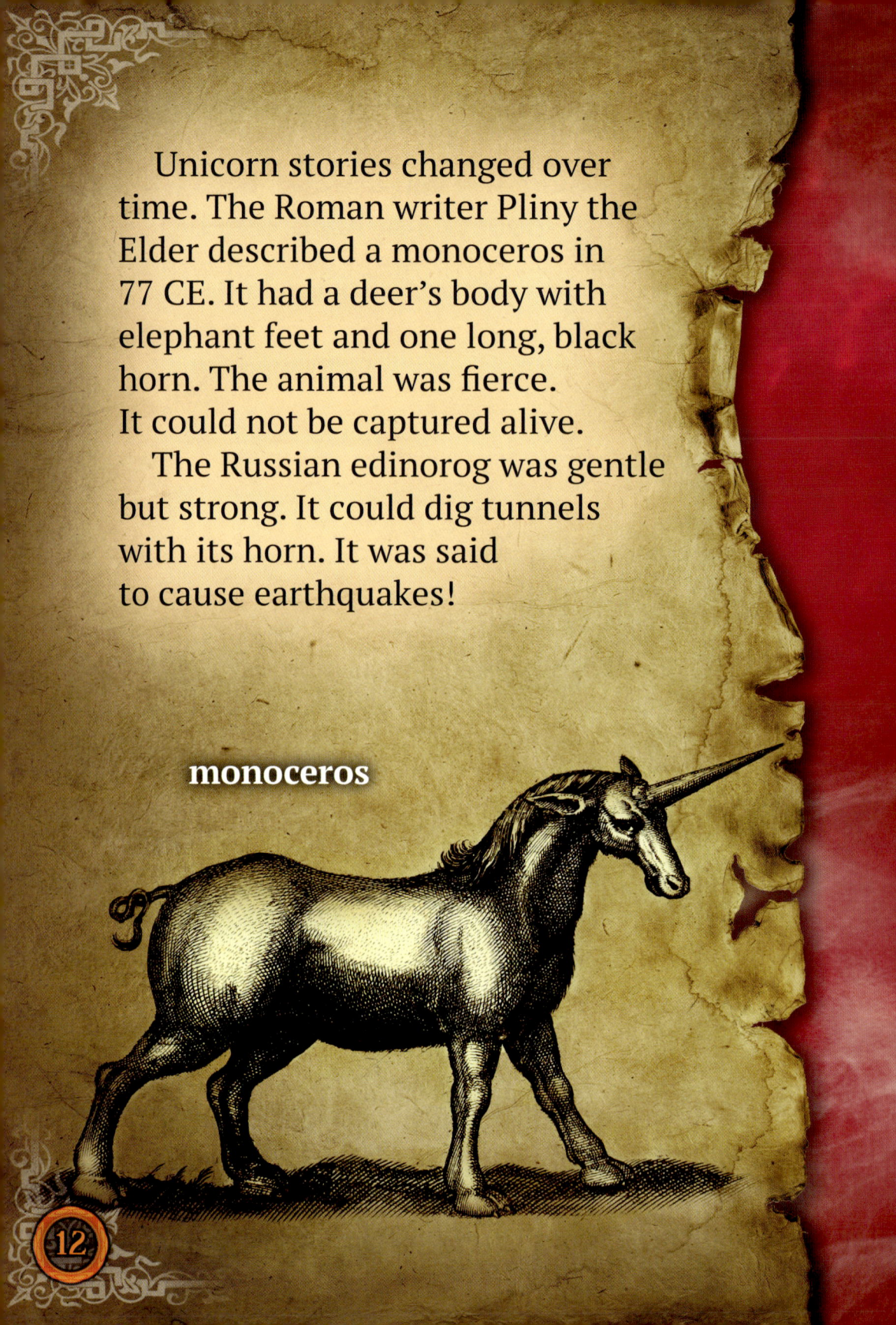

Types of Unicorns

qilin

edinorog

monoceros

Ctesias unicorn

During the **Middle Ages**, unicorns became Christian symbols of **innocence** and goodness. They became gentler. Their coats were all white.

Many people believed unicorns were real. The creatures became popular in art and **literature**. Stories about them were used to teach lessons. Paintings often showed unicorn hunts and women with unicorns.

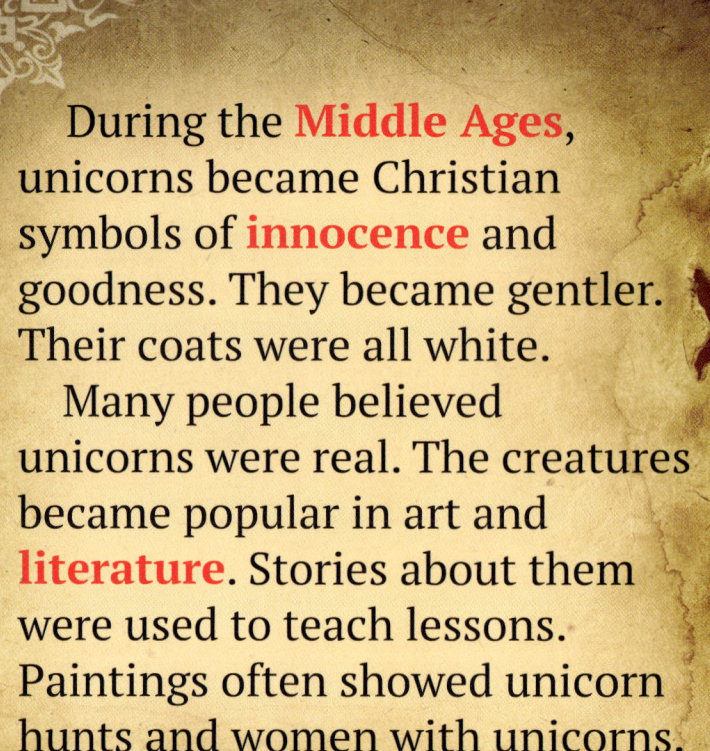

Unicorn Timeline

Around 400 BCE: Unicorn myths begin in ancient Greece and China

77 CE: Pliny the Elder writes about the monoceros in *Natural History*

Around 500 to 1500: The unicorn becomes a symbol of goodness and purity

Scientists believe other animals **inspired** unicorn myths. Long ago, people claimed narwhal **tusks** were unicorn horns.

Other animals were thought to be unicorns, too. Indian rhinos have a single horn. Aurochs and other two-horned animals appear to have one horn when viewed from the side. Animals with two horns may also break or lose a horn.

Indian rhino

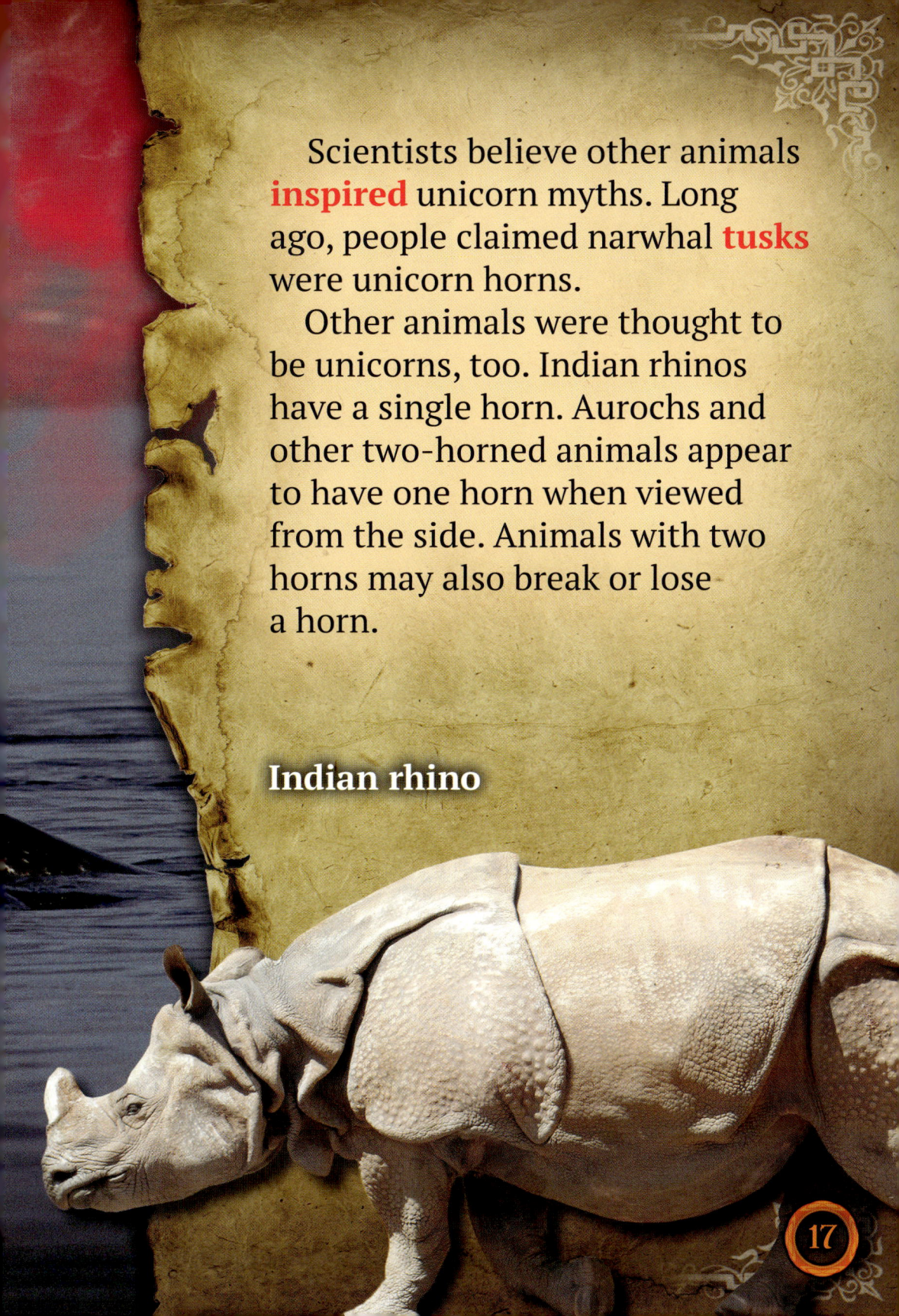

RAINBOWS AND GLITTER

Many of today's unicorns continue to be fierce. But they have also found their shine! They are often colorful and glittery. Modern unicorns are usually gentle and have magical horns.

Television, films, and books show how powerful these creatures can be. In *My Little Pony: Friendship is Magic*, the Mane 6 use the Elements of Harmony to keep their home safe.

Media Mention

Movie: *Harry Potter and the Sorcerer's Stone*

Year released: 2001

Description: Harry Potter finds out Lord Voldemort drinks unicorn blood to stay alive.

Unicorn Powers: blood keeps people alive, those who harm unicorns are cursed, unicorn hair is used in some wands

My Little Pony: Friendship is Magic

The modern unicorn offers fun, fantasy, and color. Unicorn-themed products and foods are in demand. These cheerful items are often full of glitter. They make people feel special!

The magic of unicorns has charmed people for centuries. Our love of unicorns has never been stronger or more sparkly!

GLOSSARY

betrayal—the act of breaking someone's or something's trust

enchanted—pleased or charmed

fierce—strong and intense

innocence—the state of being unaware of bad or harmful things in the world

inspired—gave someone an idea about what to do or create

literature—written works, often books, that are highly respected

mane—the long, thick hair on the head and neck of a horse or unicorn

Middle Ages—the period of European history from about 500 to 1500 CE

myths—ancient stories about the beliefs or history of a group of people; myths also try to explain events.

purity—the state of being free from evil or guilt

symbols—things that stand for something else

tame—to bring from a wild to a gentle state

tusks—long teeth that stick out of the mouths of some animals

TO LEARN MORE

AT THE LIBRARY

Meister, Cari. *Unicorns*. North Mankato, Minn.: Capstone, 2020.

Mills, Andrea. *Mythical Beasts*. New York, N.Y.: DK Publishing, 2018.

Seraphini, Temisa, and Sophie Robin. *The Secret Lives of Unicorns*. New York, N.Y.: Flying Eye Books, 2019.

ON THE WEB

FACTSURFER

Factsurfer.com gives you a safe, fun way to find more information.

1. Go to www.factsurfer.com

2. Enter "unicorns" into the search box and click 🔍.

3. Select your book cover to see a list of related content.

INDEX

appearance, 6, 10, 11, 12, 14, 18

art, 14

Asia, 10

aurochs, 17

Christian, 14

Ctesias, 11, 13

edinorog, 12, 13

Europe, 10

explanations, 17

Greek, 11, 13

Harry Potter and the Sorcerer's Stone, 19

history, 6, 9, 10, 11, 12, 14

horn, 5, 6, 9, 11, 12, 17, 18

hunters, 4, 9, 14

Indian rhinos, 17

literature, 14

Middle Ages, 9, 14

monoceros, 12, 13

My Little Pony: Friendship is Magic, 18, 19

myths, 10, 17

narwhals, 16, 17

origin, 11

Pliny the Elder, 12

powers, 5, 9, 12, 18

products, 20

qilin, 10, 13

Roman, 12, 13

Russian, 12, 13

Scotland, 6

symbols, 6, 10, 14

timeline, 14-15

tusks, 16, 17

types, 13

The images in this book are reproduced through the courtesy of: Viktoriia Bondarenko, front cover (hero); Dave Allen Photography, front cover (background); Liju Andrews Henry, pp. 2-3; Marben, p. 3 (horn); mariait, p. 4; VeronArt16, pp. 4-5; Jakub Korczyk, p. 6; Mary Evans Picture Library/ ageFotoStock, pp. 6-7; Annibale Carracci/ Wiki Commons, pp. 8-9; Chronicle/ Alamy, pp. 10-11; Smithsonian Libraries/ Wiki Commons, p. 12; Anandajoti./ Wiki Commons, p. 13 (qilin); Heinrich HarderScience/ Wiki Commons, p. 13 (edinorog); Sailko/ Wiki Commons, p. 13 (monoceros); History Images/ Alamy, p. 13 (Ctesias unicorn), 15 (middle); The Yorck Project/ Wiki Commons, p. 14; Album/ Alamy, p. 15 (top); mambo/ Alamy, p. 15 (bottom); Flip Nicklin/ Minden Picture/ SuperStock, pp. 16-17; Kletr, p. 17; Lifestyle pictures/ Alamy, pp. 18-19; Collection Christophel/ Alamy, p. 19 (top); Arina P Habich, p. 20; FamVeld, pp. 20-21; Catmando, pp. 22-24 (background), 23 (unicorn).